Teeny Tiny, the Snowflake

Learns to obey his parents

By Judy Berryhill
Illustrated by Shan Williams

Once upon a time a little snowflake lived on a big fluffy, white snow-cloud with Papa and Mama Snow.

The big cloud was full of snowflakes, and they all lived happily together as Mr. Wind blew the beautiful cloud across the big, big sky.

The little snowflake was so tiny the other snowflakes called him Teeny Tiny.

But Teeny Tiny did not mind being small. He still had just as much fun as the other snowflakes.

One day Old Man Winter arrived.

"It's time to leap off the cloud and go down to earth," he said.

The snowflakes' job on earth was to let the children play with them to make snowmen and go sleigh-riding.

All the snowflakes, except Teeny Tiny, shouted with joy and ran to the edge of the big snow-cloud.

"Come and see," they all called out as they looked down at the big earth. But Teeny Tiny was too frightened.

Finally Teeny Tiny tiptoed to the edge of the cloud where his parents were waiting.

Far below he saw snow and ice everywhere.

"I've never seen a polar bear before!" Teeny Tiny said with excitement. "They have enough snow down there in Alaska," Mr. Wind said as he blew the snow-cloud on its way.

In Utah, the tall mountains reached high into the sky.

He saw the people having lots of fun skiing through the deep, deep snow.

"They don't need us down there," said Mr. Wind and away they went.

"Mama Snow, I don't want to leap from the snow-cloud," said Teeny Tiny.

"But we must," Mama Snow replied. "That's the only way we can share our love with the children."

"But look how small I am," Teeny Tiny said, looking down at his small body.

"God does not look at the size of our bodies, but how much love we have in our heart for others," said Papa Snow.

Mr. Wind blew out a loud whistle of air and sent the snow-cloud on its way.

"We will keep looking until we find a place that needs snow," he said.

"Wow!" all the snowflakes shouted when they saw the Grand Canyon.

Even Teeny Tiny peeked over the edge of the snow-cloud.

"Ugh, it's too deep," he said, closing his eyes and turning away.

Again Mr. Wind huffed and puffed and with a mighty blow, he headed the snow-cloud westward towards California.

"Surely they will want snow there," he said.

Suddenly, they saw sunny California below them.

People were everywhere, swimming, surfing, and laying in the warm sun.

"They sure don't want us down there," Mr. Wind said, shaking his head.

Teeny Tiny laughed. He was very happy on the big snow-cloud.

By the force of Mr. Wind, the big snow-cloud was soon out of sight.

Traveling across the ocean, large, gray whales were leaping high in the water.

Large ships were sailing in both directions.

Teeny Tiny hoped that he might get to live on the snow-cloud forever.

After a long, long journey, they saw Hawaii below them.

"Oh no," cried Mr. Wind, "Hawaii never wants snow."

"We must get away from here quickly," Papa Snow said.

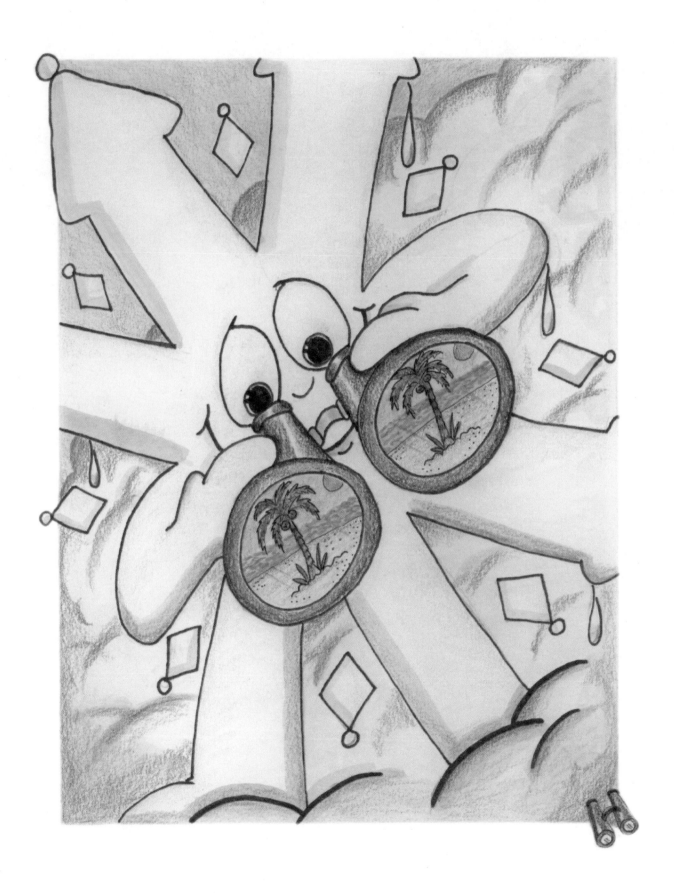

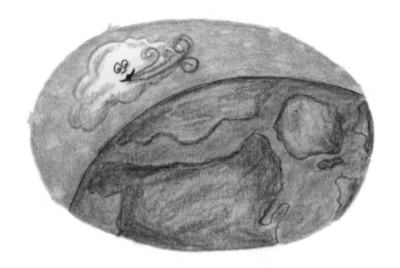

Mr. Wind moaned and groaned with a loud roar. The snow-cloud swiftly moved on across the ocean.

On around the world, the snow-cloud drifted.

The snowflakes became very sleepy and went to sleep. They slept and slept. They traveled across many countries.

All was quiet when suddenly they heard the chimes of Big Ben in London, England.

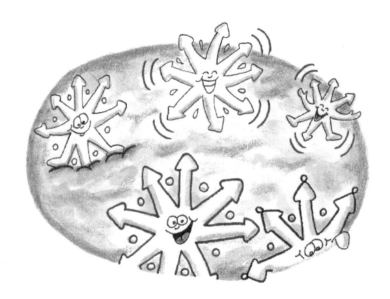

"Maybe we can leap off here!" the snowflakes shouted with glee.

But they were too late. Snow was already knee-deep there.

"We will not give up," said Mr. Wind. "We will just keep looking."

Teeny Tiny smiled. Maybe we won't be needed on earth after all, he thought.

The next morning, the skyscrapers loomed high in the New York sky. Central Park was covered with snow. Teeny Tiny giggled with delight.

By the next day, the snow-cloud had drifted south to a warmer climate. The snow-cloud looked like cotton candy under the bright sun.

All the boys and girls were looking up in the sky.

They were wishing for a big snow for Christmas.

Many had asked their parents for a sled for Christmas, but without snow, they could not go sleigh-riding.

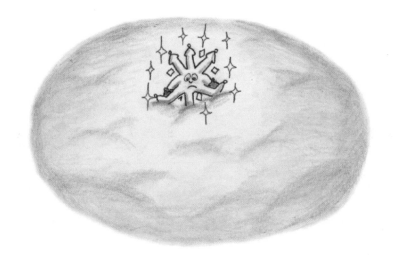

On Christmas Eve all the children were so excited.

They could hardly wait until Christmas morning to see all their gifts under the Christmas tree.

Immediately, the sparkling snowflakes began leaping from the cloud all except for Teeny Tiny. Even though he was frightened, Teeny Tiny glittered in the moonlight.

The big earth began turning white with snow.

The children were very, very happy.

"Teeny Tiny, it is time for us to jump," his parents said.

"I do not want to fall," he cried, pointing his tiny finger towards the earth.

"When we jump from the cloud, we will not fall. The wind will hold us up as we glide down to earth," said Papa Snow.

"Teeny Tiny, you must always obey your parents," his <u>mother</u> told him.

"We also must show our love by helping others," Papa Snow said.

"Look, do you see that long steep hill that has no snow?" Papa asked.

Teeny Tiny nodded.

"Without lots of snow on the hill, the children cannot sleigh-ride."

Teeny Tiny said, "But Papa, I want to live on the cloud forever."

Teeny Tiny made his parents very, very sad.

Even Teeny Tiny did not like the sad feelings he felt from the top of his little, snowy head to the tip of his tiny, snowy toes.

Mr. Wind became upset when he saw that Teeny Tiny did not obey his parents.

Mr. Wind sent one gentle puff of air across the cloud and off Teeny Tiny sailed.

Teeny Tiny screamed at the top of his little lungs and closed his eyes tightly.

Quickly his parents leaped from the snow-cloud to glide down to earth with him.

"Open your eyes, Teeny Tiny. We are having fun gliding down to earth," Mama Snow said.

Slowly, Teeny Tiny opened his eyes.

He was no longer afraid. His sad feeling was gone.

Even Papa and Mama Snow were happy.

The next morning, the children were singing Christmas carols as they gathered at the top of the hill with their new sleds.

"Come on down!" Teeny Tiny waved and called out from the bottom of the hill.

Teeny Tiny had learned two important lessons. By making others happy, he made himself happy. And from then on, Teeny Tiny would always obey his parents.

THE
END.